THE GROSS HUMAN BODY IN ACTION
AUGMENTED REALITY

# The EARS and NOSE

## A Disgusting AUGMENTED REALITY Experience

Gillia M. Olson

Lerner Publications ◆ Minneapolis

# EXPLORE THE HUMAN BODY IN BRAND-NEW WAYS WITH AUGMENTED REALITY!

1. Ask a parent or guardian for permission to download the free Lerner AR app on your digital device by going to the App Store or Google Play. When you launch the app, choose the Gross Human Body series.

Download on the App Store

GET IT ON Google Play

2. As you read, look for this icon throughout the book. It means there is an augmented reality experience on that page!

3. Use the Lerner AR app to scan the picture near the icon.

4. Watch the human body's systems come alive with augmented reality!

# CONTENTS

# INTRODUCTION
# FLESHY HEAD FLAPS

Let's talk about the fleshy flaps on your head—your ears and nose. Did you know they're connected to each other inside your head? They connect to your mouth too.

Ears and noses are distinctive parts of our faces.

Your ears and nose each have their own special gunk. Sticky earwax and gooey snot do important jobs. A lot is happening inside your head that you probably don't know about. Let's take a look.

A runny nose is annoying, but snot helps keep us healthy.

CHAPTER 1

# SOUND FUNNELS AND WAX FACTORIES: YOUR EARS

Let's face it. Ears are funny looking. They're oddly shaped flaps of skin that stick out from the sides of your head. But those weird flaps have a purpose. They funnel sound into your earholes.

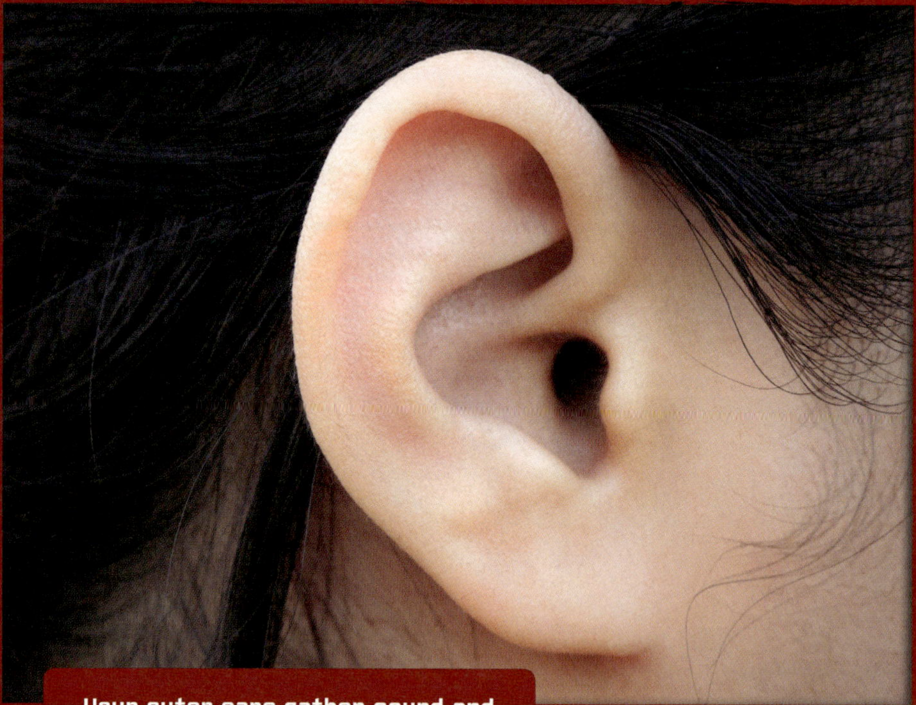

Your outer ears gather sound and direct it into your earholes.

Mixed martial arts fighters often damage their ear cartilage, which can cause bumpy scar tissue to form.

The outer ear, or pinna, is made mostly of flexible cartilage. The pinna looks strange, but it's not usually gross. That is, unless you injure it. When the pinna's cartilage gets damaged, blood may pool in the affected area. This blocks fresh blood from reaching your cartilage. Without fresh blood, cartilage gets infected and dies. Thick, uneven scar tissue forms around the area. Eventually, your ear can look like lumpy, bumpy cauliflower.

The earhole is the beginning of the ear canal. Besides bringing sound into your head, your ear canals keep dust and germs out. They do this by creating sticky, stinky earwax.

Without earwax, dust and germs would fly deep into your head, leading to infections and other problems.

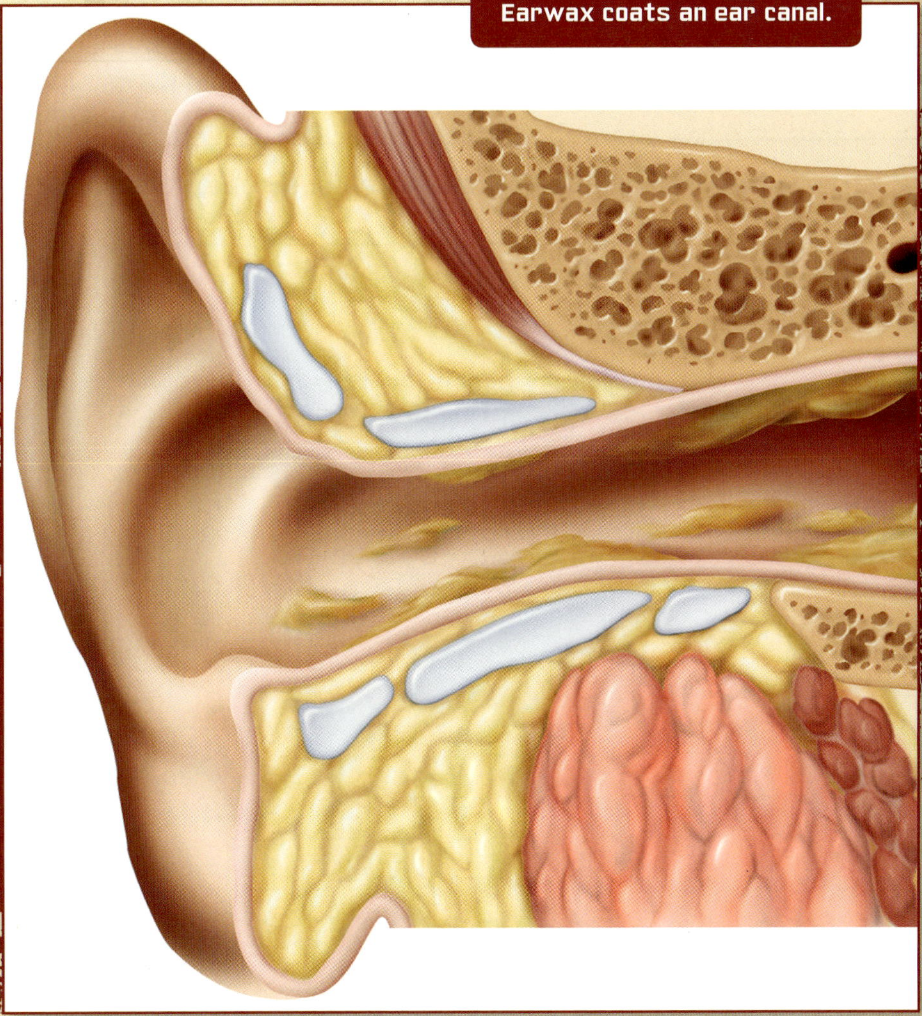

Earwax coats an ear canal.

Glands inside your ear canals make earwax. It gets its stickiness from fat. Sticky wax traps flying particles to keep them from getting deeper into your head. It also gets rid of dead ear skin. As your jaw moves, earwax moves to the entrances of your ear canals. It takes out the ear trash.

People have different kinds of earwax. The dry type is flaky and light brown or gray. Wet earwax is honey brown or orange and has a stronger smell. Bonus: People with strong-smelling wax tend to have more body odor too!

Wet earwax

Earwax is always moving out of your ear canals, so cleaning your outer ears is important.

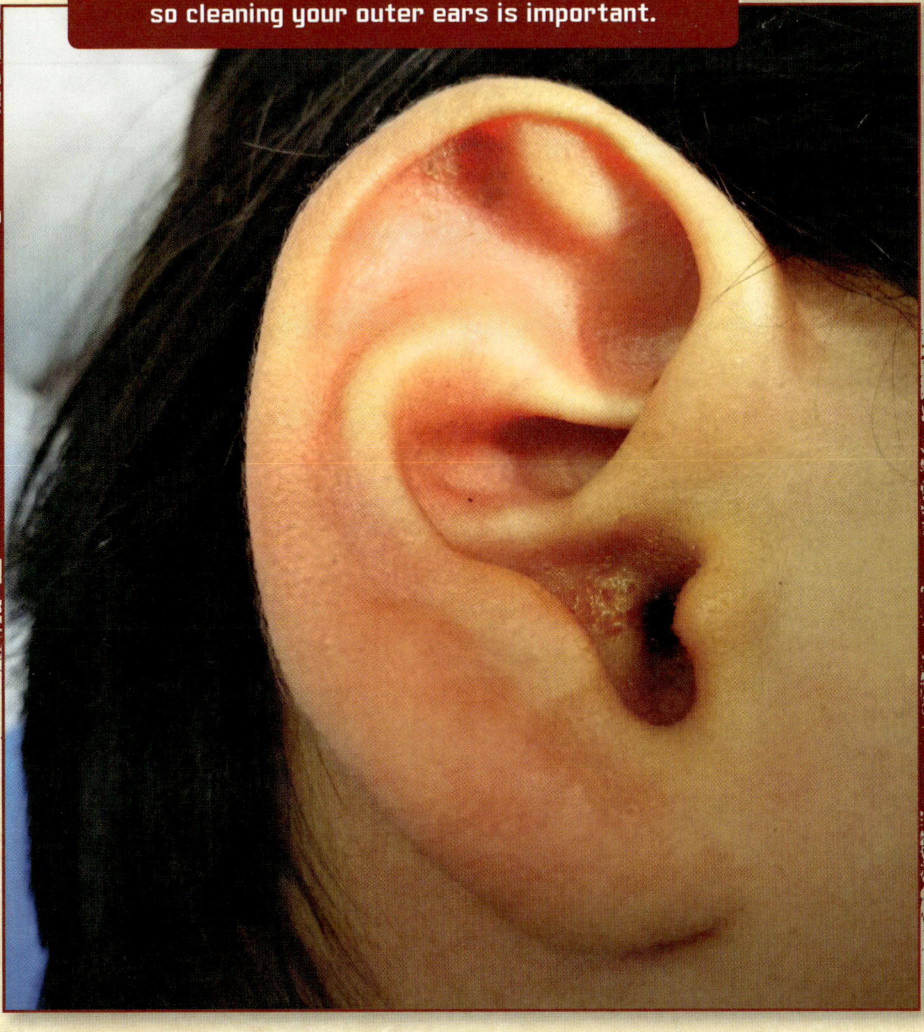

Usually earwax does its job without much fuss. But sometimes, it forms a blockage in your ear canal. Then you might have to see a doctor. You might get drops in your ear to soften the wax so it comes out on its own. Or the doctor might take it out with a hooked tool. Yikes!

CHAPTER 2

# FEELING DIZZY: EAR PROBLEMS

Sound travels down your ear canals until it reaches your eardrums. The eardrum's thin tissue vibrates like a drum when sounds hit it. The middle ear is on the other side of the eardrum. This small area is covered with mucus.

Sounds hits the round surface of the eardrum, causing the tissue to vibrate.

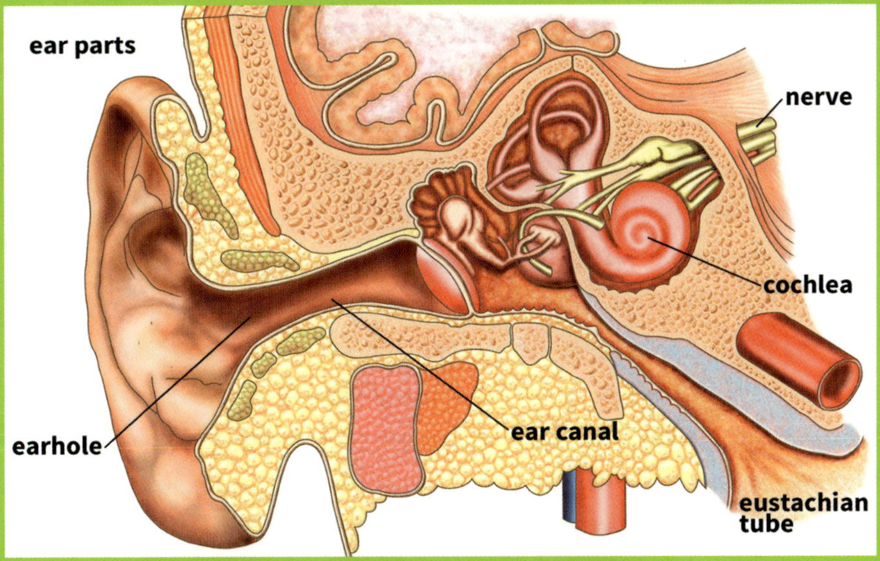


The ear has many parts that work together to allow us to hear.

Three small bones transfer sound vibrations from your middle ear to your inner ear. The inner ear's cochlea looks like a tiny snail shell. The cochlea turns sound vibrations into signals to send to your brain.

Eustachian tubes connect your middle ears to your nose. Sometimes, fluid from your nose gets into the tubes and reaches the middle ears, which can cause ear infections. Eustachian tubes also help with balance. That's why ear infections can make you feel dizzy.

If you have a fungal infection in your ear canals, you probably need to see a doctor.

Fungus may grow in ear canals. Otomycosis is a common fungal infection for people who live in warm, wet places. Swimmers who get water in their ears can get it too. The infection causes smelly fluid to drain from the ears. The fluid can be white, green, yellow, or even black—yuck! This nasty fungal infection needs to be treated by a doctor.

Some ear diseases can damage hearing. Meniere's disease affects the inner ear, causing severe dizziness and hearing loss. Otosclerosis makes the bones in the middle ear grow incorrectly, leading to hearing problems.

Dizziness is often linked to inner ear problems.

CHAPTER 3

# BOOGER PEARLS: YOUR NOSE

If you think about it, the lump of flesh and cartilage in the middle of your face is pretty amazing. Your nose can smell more than one trillion scents, including roses, fresh-cut grass, and cheesy pizza. But not everything you smell is pleasant. Sweaty socks and garbage produce strong odors. And sometimes there's no escaping the smell of nasty farts.

The strong smell of flowers attracts bees and other pollinators.

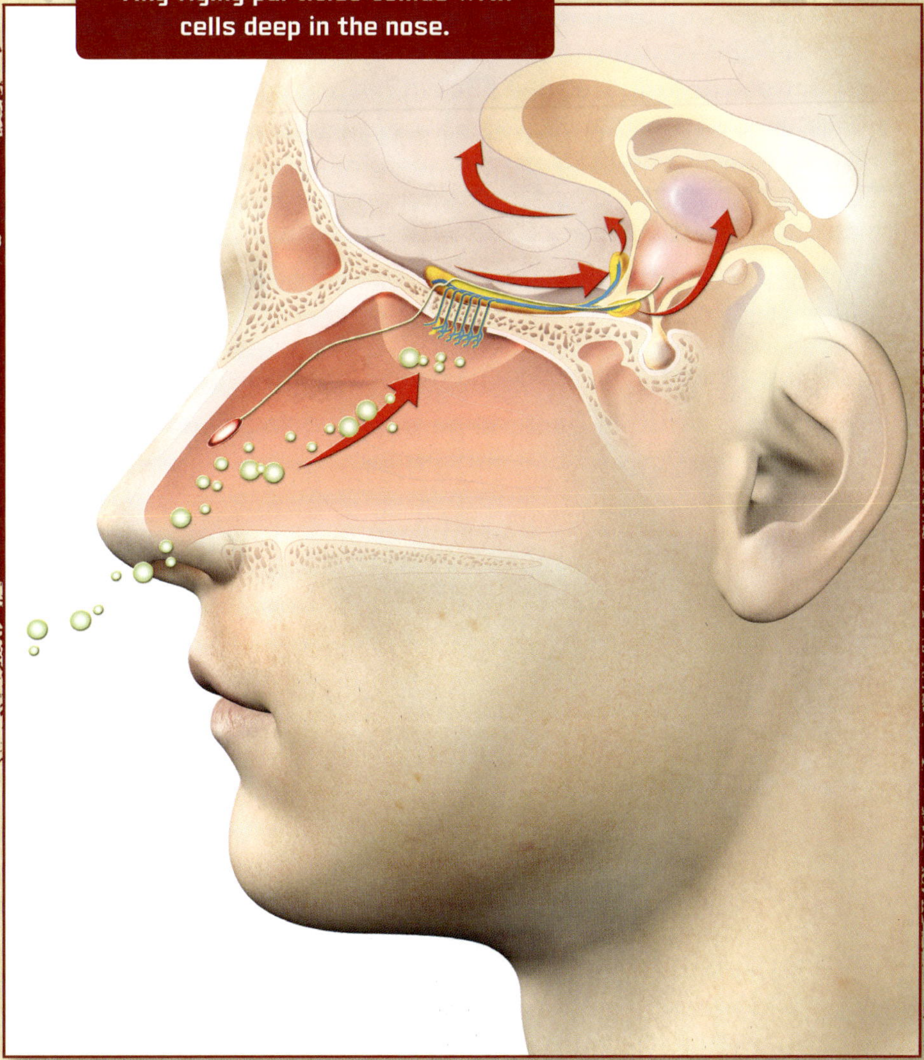

Tiny flying particles collide with cells deep in the nose.

When you smell something, it means microscopic particles are flying into your nose. So when you sniff the garbage you should have taken out last week, you're inhaling tiny pieces of rotten trash. The particles hit special cells in the back of your nose that send information about the smell to your brain.

Your nose does more than suck in particles for you to smell. It warms the air going into your lungs. It also traps germs with sticky mucus.

Mucus is mostly water mixed with small amounts of salt, dead tissue cells, and mucin. Mucin is a substance that makes mucus sticky. In 1921, scientist Alexander Fleming discovered that mucin kills bacteria. Mucus from Fleming's runny nose dripped into a dish of bacteria he was studying. Over the next two weeks, the mucus killed the bacteria.

When you have a cold, your mucus production goes into overdrive.

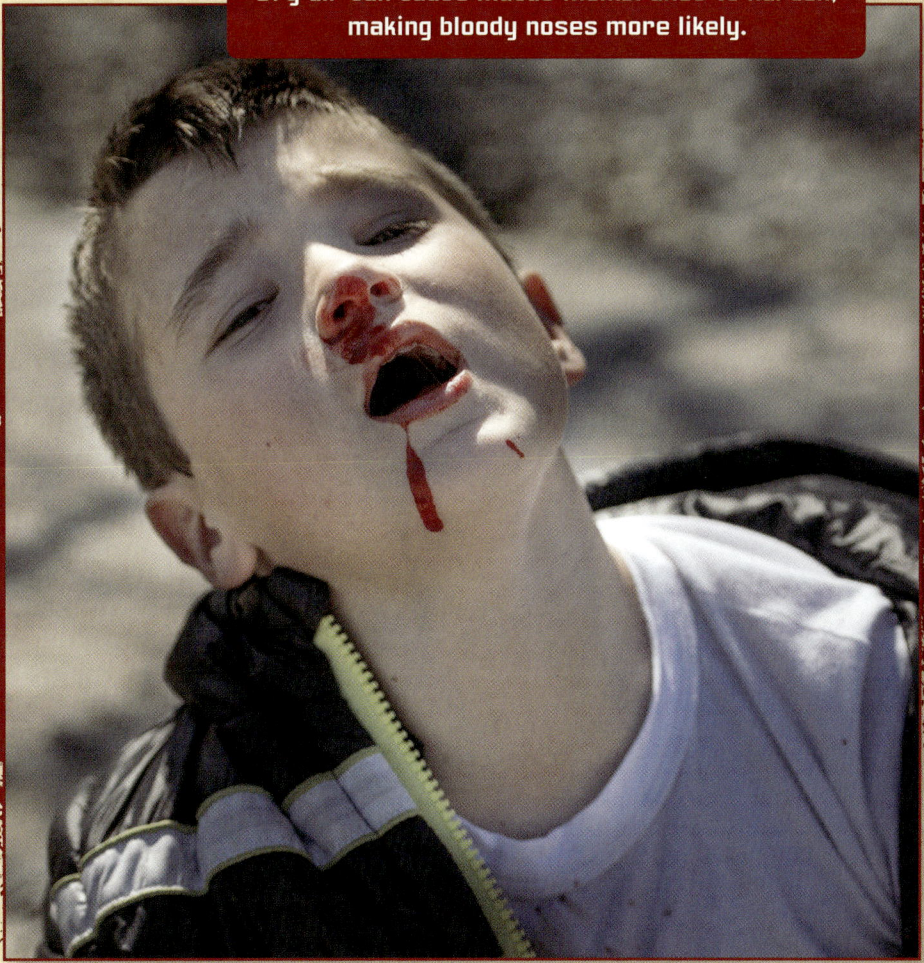

Dry air can cause mucus membranes to harden, making bloody noses more likely.

Mucus is produced by mucous membranes. Mucous membranes are found in your mouth, nose, and anywhere the outside of your body meets the inside. If the mucous membranes in your nose get too dry, they can get hard and crusty. Then you might get a bloody nose if you wipe or blow it too hard.

This illustration shows blue mucus-making cells surrounded by cilia.

Your mucous membranes make 4 to 6 cups of mucus every day. Most of it runs down your throat without you even noticing it. If it didn't, it would constantly flow from your nose and mouth. No one wants that.

People often use different names for mucus depending on its consistency and where it's produced. Runny snot comes from your nose. Sticky phlegm is mucus from your throat that you may cough up when you have a cold.

Boogers are pieces of dried mucus in your nose that can develop while you're breathing dry air. They also form around germs or other particles the nose traps, similar to the way clams form pearls around grains of sand inside their shells. That makes boogers nose pearls! You probably shouldn't make a necklace with them, though.

When we sneeze, we blow out mucus and the dust and germs it has trapped.

Mucus does such a good job trapping germs that when you swallow mucus, you swallow a lot of germs too. Luckily, your stomach acid kills them. Sometimes, though, the germs grab onto your throat, settle in, and start making more germs. That's often how a cold starts.

About two hundred different viruses cause colds. If your mucus misses a virus and it gets inside your body, it's up to your immune system to kill it. One way your immune system responds is by making more mucus to flush out the virus. The extra mucus irritates the nose and throat, causing them to produce even more mucus. That's why you feel like a snot faucet when you have a cold.

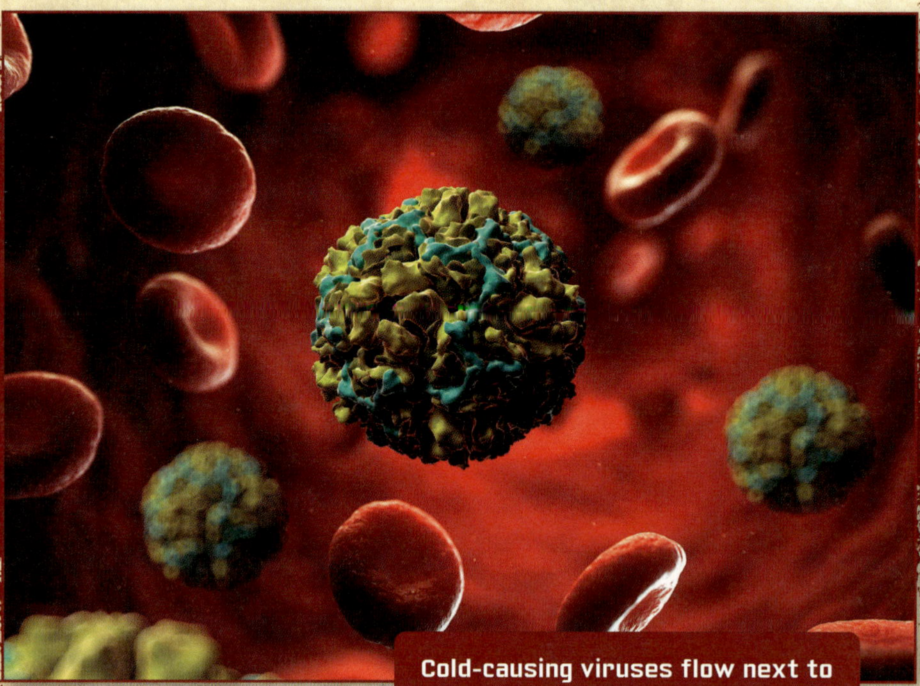

Cold-causing viruses flow next to red blood cells in the nose.

Your snot can tell you a lot about your health. White boogers mean your nose is dry. When you have a cold, white blood cells fight the invading virus. They turn green when they die, making your snot a lovely yellow-green color. Brown or black snot might mean you breathed in dust or dirt. But sometimes dark mucus indicates a fungal infection.

The next time you blow your nose, check the color of the snot for information about your health.

CHAPTER 4

# EMPTY HEADS AND NOSE FUR: YOUR SINUSES

Did you know your head has a lot of empty space? That might sound like a problem, but don't worry. Everyone's head is full of air. You have eight hollow spaces, or sinuses, in the bones of your skull. Your sinuses produce germ-trapping mucus. They also make our heads lighter and change the sound of our voices.

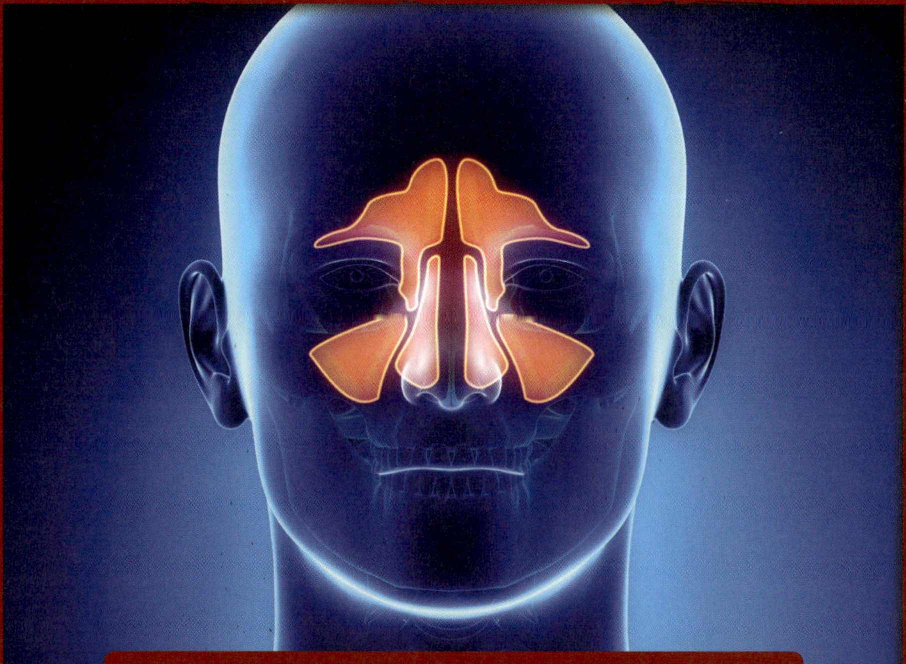

Without sinuses, our voices would sound different and we'd probably get sick more often.

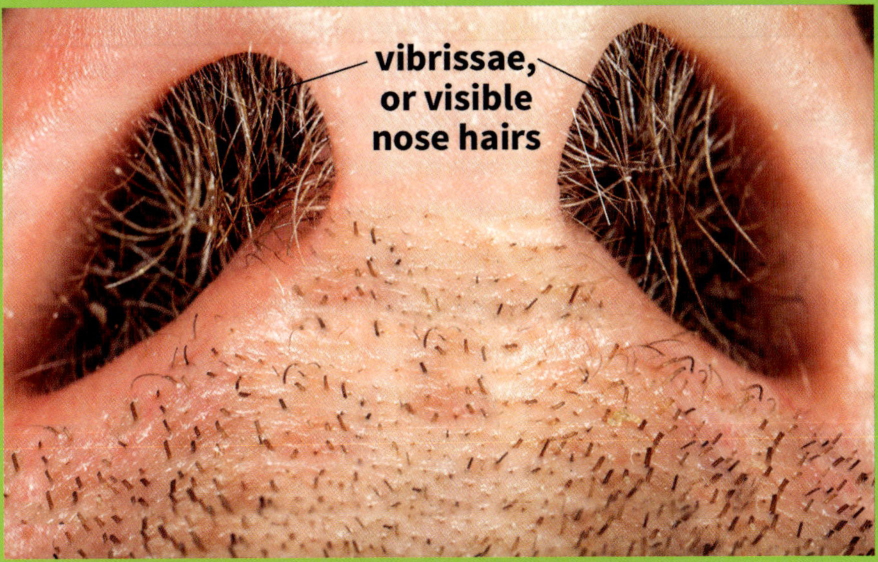


Adults have longer and thicker nose hair than kids have.

Your sinuses and air passages are covered in microscopic hairs called cilia. Cilia move in waves, pushing mucus around and keeping your passages clear. They look like tiny worms in your head.

Vibrissae are the nose hairs you can see without a microscope. They catch germs and particles that fly into your nose. Don't pluck those valuable hairs! Pulling one out leaves a wound where germs can enter your body, possibly leading to a nasty infection.

Many things can affect your nose and sinuses besides germs. People born with cystic fibrosis produce mucus that is too thick and sticky. The mucus clogs airways and can damage the lungs and other organs. Thick mucus makes it easier for germs to grow, so people with cystic fibrosis often get infections.

Sometimes your immune system mistakes a harmless substance for an invader. Allergies send mucus production into overdrive, potentially causing breathing problems. Common allergens include animal hair, peanuts, and plant pollen.

Many people are allergic to cats.

Allergy symptoms can make you feel as if you have a cold.

Mucus, nose hair, and earwax can be nasty, but they help keep us healthy. So the next time you blow out a glob of snot or wipe off a chunk of earwax, be thankful for your sticky little helpers. Nose pearls are valuable after all!

# GROSS EARS AND NOSE FACTS

- The average adult human ear is 2.5 inches (6.4 cm) long.
- The world's longest nose is 3.46 inches (8.79 cm) from the bridge to the tip.
- A person's cilia can keep moving for up to twenty hours after death.
- A sneeze can send one hundred thousand germs into the air.
- People with certain medical conditions may experience hyperosmia, or an increased sense of smell.
- Each year, about twelve million people visit the doctor for earwax problems.

# GLOSSARY

**allergy:** sneezing, itching, or a rash caused by a substance that doesn't have the same effect on most people

**bacteria:** tiny living things that live all around and inside you

**cartilage:** a flexible tissue in the body

**fungus:** a plantlike organism such as a mushroom, mold, or rust

**immune system:** the system that protects the body against disease and infection

**infection:** a sickness caused by bacteria or a virus

**microscopic:** invisible without a microscope

**mucin:** a substance in mucus that makes it sticky and kills bacteria

**mucus:** a thick, slippery liquid made by the body

**sinus:** a hollow space in the bones of the head

**vibrissa:** a visible hair in the nose

**virus:** a microscopic organism that can cause disease

# FURTHER INFORMATION

Ear Facts for Kids
https://www.coolkidfacts.com/ear-facts/

Everything You Didn't Want to Know about Snot
https://www.pbs.org/video/everything-you-didnt-want-to-know-about-snot-ivtlso/

Farndon, John. *Tiny Killers: When Bacteria and Viruses Attack*. Minneapolis: Hungry Tomato, 2017.

How Different Diseases Make You Smell
https://www.pbs.org/video/gross-science-death-dragon-worms/

Interesting Nose Facts
https://www.coolkidfacts.com/nose-facts/

Leed, Percy. *The Mouth (A Nauseating Augmented Reality Experience)*. Minneapolis: Lerner Publications, 2021.

Macdonald, Fiona. *The Science of Snot and Phlegm: The Slimy Truth about Breathing*. New York: Franklin Watts, 2018.

Rajczak Nelson, Kristen. *What Is Earwax Made Of? And Other FAQs about Your Body*. New York: Gareth Stevens, 2017.

# INDEX



# PHOTO ACKNOWLEDGMENTS

Image credits: Freer/Shutterstock.com, p. 2 (bottom); adamkaz/Getty Images, p. 4; seksan Mongkhonkhamsaoy/Getty Images, p. 5; Kwangmoozaa/Getty Images, p. 6; Jeff Bottari/Zuffa LLC/Getty Images, p. 7; Westend61/Getty Images, p. 8; Brian Evans/Getty Images, p. 9; rob_lan/Getty Images, p. 10; KOHYAO/Shutterstock .com, p. 11; Designua/Shutterstock.com, p. 12; Stocktrek Images/Getty Images, p. 13; LWA/Dann Tardif/Getty Images, p. 14; BlurryMe/Shutterstock.com, p. 15; Leland Bobbe/Getty Images, p. 16; Axel_Kock/Shutterstock.com, p. 17; Suwan Wanawattanawong/Shutterstock.com, p. 18; Stratos Giannikos/Shutterstock.com, p. 19; Nanoclustering/Science Photo Library/Getty Images, p. 20; PaulGregg/Getty Images, p. 21; SCIEPRO/Science Photo Library/Getty Images, p. 22; Oleg Golovnev/ Shutterstock.com, p. 23; CLIPAREA/Custom Media/Shutterstock.com, p. 24; Vera Larina/Shutterstock.com, p. 25; Jaromir Chalabala/Shutterstock.com, p. 26; Lucidio Studio Inc/Getty Images, p. 27. Design elements: amtitus/Getty Images; Anastasiia_M/Getty Images; arthobbit/Getty Images; atakan/Getty Images; cajoer/ Getty Images; desifoto/Getty Images; EduardHarkonen/Getty Images; enjoynz/ Getty Images; Eratel/Getty Images; gadost/Getty Images; kaylabutler/Getty Images; Yevhenii Dubinko/Getty Images.

Cover images: wildpixel/Getty Images (nose); 1FreeGetty Images (slime).

Lerner Publications Company
An imprint of Lerner Publishing Group, Inc.
241 First Avenue North
Minneapolis, MN 55401 USA

For reading levels and more information, look up this title at www.lernerbooks.com.

Main body text set in Aptifer Sans LT Pro.
Typeface provided by Linotype AG.

**Designer:** Kimberly Morales **Photo Editor:** Cynthia Zemlicka

**Library of Congress Cataloging-in-Publication Data**

The Cataloging-in-Publication Data for *The Ears and Nose (A Disgusting Augmented Reality Experience)* is on file at the Library of Congress.
ISBN 978-1-5415-9810-2 (lib. bdg.)
ISBN 978-1-72841-427-0 (pbk.)
ISBN 978-1-72840-133-1 (eb pdf)

Manufactured in the United States of America
1-48001-48679-2/12/2020